# Magic
## Animal Friends

For Holly and Monster,
our own fluffyfaces!

## Special thanks to Valerie Wilding

ORCHARD BOOKS

First published in Great Britain in 2017 by The Watts Publishing Group

1 3 5 7 9 10 8 6 4 2

Text copyright © Working Partners Ltd 2017
Illustrations copyright © Working Partners Ltd 2017
Series created by Working Partners Ltd

A CIP catalogue record for this book is available from the British Library.

ISBN 978 1 40834 422 4

Printed in Great Britain

The paper and board used in this book are made from wood from responsible sources

Orchard Books
An imprint of Hachette Children's Group
Part of The Watts Publishing Group Limited
Carmelite House, 50 Victoria Embankment, London EC4Y 0DZ

An Hachette UK Company
www.hachette.co.uk
www.hachettechildrens.co.uk

# Ava Fluffyface's Special Day

Daisy Meadows

ORCHARD

Brighteyes' Home

Spelltop School

Treehouse

Picnic Area

Twinkling Inkwell

Honey Tree

Sunshine Meadow

# Map of Friendship Forest

Library

Playground

Greenhouse

School Hall

Madame Doodleflap's House

Can you keep a secret? I thought you could!

Then I'll tell you about an enchanted wood.

It lies through the door in the old oak tree,

Let's go there now - just follow me!

We'll find adventure that never ends,

And meet the Magic Animal Friends!

Love,
Goldie the Cat

# Contents

CHAPTER ONE

# Grizelda Makes a Wicked Plan

"What a beautiful speckled shell," said
Lily Hart, gazing at the bird's egg in her
hand.

"I've never seen such a pretty shade of
blue," said her best friend, Jess Forester.
She turned to Lily's mother. "Do you

 9

think it'll hatch, Mrs Hart?"

Mr and Mrs Hart were vets. They ran the Helping Paw Wildlife Hospital from the converted barn at the bottom of their garden. The girls were in the barn, showing Lily's mum their find. A curious little rabbit and a hedgehog with a hurt paw peered at them from hutches nearby.

Mrs Hart placed the egg in a box under a heat lamp. "There's a very good chance it'll hatch," she said. "It will be as warm as a nest in here."

"I can't wait!" declared Lily.

Lily and Jess loved helping with the

animals, and the days when new babies
were born were extra special.

"It's lucky you spotted the egg, Lily,"
said Jess.

"It was in the long grass next to the
rescued guinea pigs," said Lily. "I think it
fell from the apple tree there. I searched
for the nest but I couldn't find it."

"I need to look at the lamb with the sore foot," said Mrs Hart. "I'll be back soon." She checked the heat lamp once more and went out.

Lily tucked her dark hair behind her ears and gazed at the egg on its soft bed. "What sort of bird will you be?" she whispered.

Suddenly the girls heard a miaow behind them.

A beautiful cat with golden fur and sparkling green eyes

was sitting in the doorway.

"Goldie!" cried Jess.

The girls stroked Goldie's soft fur. She purred and rubbed happily against their legs.

"This must mean we're off to Friendship Forest!" cried Lily.

Lily and Jess had an incredible secret. Whenever Goldie appeared, she led them to a magical forest where the animals lived in cute little houses among the trees. And something even more amazing happened there. All the animals in Friendship Forest could talk!

"We can visit our friends and be back before the egg hatches," said Jess.

No time passed in the real world while they were in Friendship Forest. It was all part of the magic.

Goldie bounded out of the barn and the girls followed. They jumped across the stepping stones across Brightley Stream and ran through Brightley Meadow towards an old oak tree with bare, dead branches.

As they reached it, the tree sprang to life. Glossy green leaves sprouted from every twig, and robins and kingfishers played between them. In the grass below, yellow daffodils popped up, opening their trumpety petals to the sun. Bright blue dragonflies darted around and bumblebees buzzed among the blooms.

Goldie touched the tree trunk with her paw and two familiar words appeared in the bark. Lily and Jess shared an excited smile. They held hands and together they read the words aloud.

"Friendship Forest!"

Immediately a small door appeared in the trunk. Lily turned the leaf-shaped handle and pushed it open.

Shimmering golden light flooded out. The girls followed Goldie through the door, ducking their heads. A tingly feeling sizzled over them and they knew that meant that they were shrinking, just a little. When the glow faded, they were in a grassy clearing surrounded by tall

trees. Warm sunbeams filtered through
the leaves, making the light dance on
pretty primroses in the grass. Birds sang in
the branches above and the river nearby
gurgled happily.

Goldie was standing on her hind legs,
wearing a glittery scarf around her neck.

"Hello, girls," she said.

Lily and Jess gave her a big hug.

"It's lovely to see you again," said Lily.

"I've fetched you for a very special
reason," said Goldie. "I'm inviting you
to—" She broke off in alarm. In the
distance, an orb of yellow-green light had

appeared. It burst into a shower of nasty-
smelling sparks. When they'd cleared, an
ugly witch stood under the trees.

"Oh no!" cried Jess. "It's Grizelda."

Grizelda was a mean witch who was
always trying to get the animals out of
Friendship Forest so she could have it for
herself. So far, Lily and Jess had managed
to stop her, but she always came back.

The witch stomped through the forest,
snapping twigs and crushing flowers with
her black high-heeled boots. Her cloak
flew up behind her like bat wings. Her
scrawny arms poked out from her purple

tunic and her green hair was as slimy
as pondweed. A young pink flamingo
followed, squawking loudly.

"I've told you a hundred times, Banjo,"
Grizelda shrieked at him. "Stop making
that racket. You're too noisy!"

"KWARK!" screeched the flamingo.
"I'm not noisy! KWARK!"

Lily, Jess and Goldie blocked the witch's
path.

"What are you up to, Grizelda?" asked
Goldie bravely.

"I might have known you tiresome
threesome would be around," snapped

Grizelda. "I have a clever plan. When I'm done, every stupid animal in Friendship Forest will be rushing to leave. It will soon be mine, all mine!" She threw back her head and gave a harsh cackle.

"Hers, all hers!" squawked Banjo. "AK AK AK!"

He laughed so loudly that Goldie and the girls covered their ears.

"Now get out of my way!" Grizelda said. She swept past them and headed off with Banjo.

 21

"KWARK," they heard Banjo shout. "THEY'LL NEVER WORK OUT YOUR SNEAKY PLAN ... THE SCHOOL—"

"Be quiet, you silly bird!" bellowed Grizelda. She snapped her fingers and they both disappeared in a shower of crackling sparks.

Jess looked in horror at Lily and Goldie. "Grizelda's planning to cause trouble at Spelltop School again!" she gasped.

Goldie's green eyes were wide with worry. "We must get there at once."

# CHAPTER TWO

# A Nasty Tune

Goldie led them through the forest at a run. Honeybirds sang to them and the leaves rustling in the breeze made a sweet melody. Mrs Twinkletail the mouse waved from the doorway of her cottage as they raced past.

Soon they came to the pretty thatched

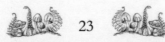

school building, much bigger than the
cottages they'd passed. Pink-and-white
blossoms surrounded the windows and
doors, the walls were covered in roses
and a bluebell hung on the roof, ready
to ring out the time. The playground was
full of toys and climbing frames and on
the other side stood the brightly painted
school library with its book-shaped roof.
A sign decorated with cheerful stars said
"Spelltop School".

"Everything looks perfect," panted Jess.
"Grizelda can't be here yet!"

"Phew!" said Lily, feeling very relieved.

"But we must warn the teachers that she's on her way."

"We'll find everyone in the hall," said Goldie. "Something special is happening there. It's the reason that I brought you to the forest today."

As Goldie led them inside, beautiful music filled the air.

"What a lovely tune!" gasped Jess.

Goldie pushed open the door to the school hall and the music grew louder. A wonderful sight met their eyes.

At one end of the hall was a stage, with purple velvet curtains pulled open.

The stage was full of pupils playing

musical instruments. Rosie Gigglepip

the guinea pig and Emily Prickleback

the hedgehog had clarinets. Chloe

Slipperslide the otter was holding a

silver trumpet in her webbed paws while

Poppy Muddlepup played a pretty pink harp. Others had violins and cellos and the three Nibblesqueak hamsters were beating perfect time on big round drums. An elderly goose in a blue waistcoat full of bulging pockets stood in front of them with his wooden conductor's stick. It was Professor Gogglewing.

When he saw the girls he put down his baton. "Welcome, Lily and Jess," he said with a big smile. "Goldie told me you'd be coming to our concert."

"So that's the surprise," exclaimed Lily in delight.

All the little animals squeaked happily.
"Our students have been practising
very hard," Professor Gogglewing told
them. "The concert is for everyone in
Friendship Forest."

"I can't wait!" cried Jess.

"But we must warn you, Headmaster,"
Lily whispered so that the young animals
wouldn't hear and get scared. "Grizelda's
plotting a nasty trick for the school."

"We can't have that!" declared Professor
Gogglewing. "Professor Cutiepaws will
arrive soon to take over the rehearsal.
When she does I'll go and make sure

Grizelda's nowhere around."

A cute little kitten bounded down from the stage.

"Hello, Lily and Jess," she squeaked, her eyes growing round with excitement. "I'm Ava Fluffyface and I've always wanted to meet you."

Lily and Jess exchanged a smile. Ava was delightful.

"What instrument do you

play, Ava?" asked Lily.

"The flute," said Ava proudly. "I made it myself from a reed. But my favourite hobby is writing songs. The orchestra's going to play one of them in the concert – and I'm going to sing. My parents are coming! I want everything to be perfect."

The hall door flew open and a white cat came running in, tripping over her tail in her hurry. She was carrying a shiny black conductor's stick.

Lily and Jess smiled. They were so pleased to see Professor Cutiepaws, the adorable, clumsy teacher.

"Sorry I'm late, Headmaster," she panted, smoothing down her long fur and straightening the pink ribbon on her head. "I got my baton caught in my classroom door. I'm such a silly sausage!"

"Well, I'm glad you're here now, Professor Cutiepaws," said Professor Gogglewing. "I'm going to take a look outside." He lowered his voice. "Grizelda's trying to

make trouble again."

"Then you must go straight away!" exclaimed the white cat. She jumped as she suddenly spotted Lily and Jess. "Goodness me!" she exclaimed. "You're forever popping up!" She gave a quick smile. "Of course, it's always lovely to see my favourite girlie-whirlies."

"We're really looking forward to the orchestra playing Ava's song," said Jess.

"Goodie!" Professor Cutiepaws skipped happily. "We'll practise that one first."

Ava hurried on to the stage and the teacher waved her baton.

 32

The orchestra began to play. The most wonderful lilting notes filled the hall. The flutes played such a beautiful melody that it made the girls tingle from head to foot. Now the drums joined in with a gentle beat. Polly Muddlepup added the sweetest tune on her harp. Professor Cutiepaws conducted them all with her baton.

But as Ava was about to sing, something very odd happened. The instruments started making dreadful screeching sounds.

"What's happening?" wailed Chloe Slipperside. "My trumpet sounds nasty."

"I can't play the right notes either!" cried Emily Prickleback, staring at her clarinet in alarm.

"Don't stop, kiddiwinkies!" called Professor Cutiepaws. "We'll get it right if we keep practising." Her baton was a black whirl as she beat the time.

But the sound was getting worse. The violins screeched and the drums thundered. The girls' hands flew to their ears to block out the horrible noise. Professor Cutiepaws tapped her baton frantically to stop the orchestra. "Bless my whiskers," she exclaimed. "Whatever's

happening?"

The players looked around at each other with frightened faces.

"Are our instruments broken?" asked Rosie Gigglepip in a wobbly voice.

Big tears spilled down Ava's fluffy cheeks. "My tune sounded horrible."

Lily and Jess put their arms around her.

"That wasn't your tune," said Lily.

"It was lovely before everything went strange," Jess assured her.

"Lily, Jess!" called Goldie. "Look, there's something very odd going on."

Goldie was pointing to the music in front of Professor Cutiepaws. The notes were wriggling and squirming. Suddenly, they jumped off the pages! They whizzed round the hall, before swooping low over their heads and flying out of the window.

"My music!" cried Ava. "It's gone!"

# CHAPTER THREE

# Magic Music

Lily and Jess dashed to the window but the notes had vanished.

"It's as if the music's under an evil spell," gasped Jess.

"Grizelda's the only person who would do that," said Lily.

"Grizelda!" exclaimed Professor

Cutiepaws.

"It has to be her," said Goldie. "But how? Professor Gogglewing would have seen her if she'd tried to sneak in."

"It's a very clever spell," said Professor Cutiepaws, holding open another book. The pages were blank. "It's stolen all the music and spoiled the instruments."

"We can't have the concert now!" sobbed Ava.

"There are

more music books in the school library,"
said Jess. "Let's ask Professor Wiggly the
librarian for help."

"Good thinking," said Lily.

Ava dried her eyes with a paw. "Can I
come too?" she asked.

"Of course you can," said Lily.

"Don't go, my lovelies!" Professor
Cutiepaws called. "It might not be safe."

"It's kind of you to worry about us,
Professor Cutiepaws," said Lily. "But we
must stop Grizelda."

Ava led them towards a door where
alphabet bricks spelled out "Welcome to

39

our library". They hurried inside.

Even though Lily and Jess had seen the library before, it still gave them a warm glow to look at the bright bookshelves and the snuggly cushions scattered round the room. The librarian was sitting at his desk, sorting library cards.

He saw the girls and wiggled over to them. "Lily and Jess, how lovely to see you!" he exclaimed. "And Goldie and Ava too ..." He looked at their worried faces. "Is something the matter?"

"Grizelda's stolen our music for the concert," explained Ava.

Jess held out the blank pages.

"And she's spoiled the instruments too," added Goldie.

"Oh dear, oh dear!" murmured the librarian, peering at the sheets through his round glasses, his forehead creased in a worried frown. "It's not just the concert Grizelda has spoiled," he said solemnly. "It's much worse than that."

"Worse!" gasped Goldie. The girls could hear a wobble of fear in her voice.

"She's begun to steal all the sound from Friendship Forest," said the librarian.

"We won't let her," Jess reassured Ava,

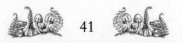

who was trembling.

"We'll do anything to beat that nasty witch!" declared Lily.

"And I'm going to help," said Ava, putting her chin up bravely. "Grizelda's not taking our lovely sounds!"

"Well said, Ava!" declared the librarian. He picked up a golden bookmark and waved it in circles. A blue book covered in pictures of sparkling musical instruments floated down into Ava's paws.

"This is a special piece of magic music," Professor Wiggly explained. "It uses every note in the forest to make a perfect tune.

When the orchestra plays it, each note that Grizelda stole will come flying back."

Ava's head drooped sadly. "But, Professor, we can't play our instruments!"

"I'm afraid this spell will have ruined all the instruments in the whole forest, not just the school," said Professor Wiggly sadly. "You will have to make some new instruments."

Ava looked stunned. "But we'll never be

able to make proper instruments. They
will all sound dreadful!"

Jess gave her a cuddle. "You said
you made your flute from a reed, Ava,
remember?"

"B-but that took ages," Ava sniffed, "I
worked on it for days."

"I'm sure we can do it, if we work
together," said Lily, "We must try."

"If you don't lift this spell soon, all the
sounds in Friendship Forest will disappear
for ever!" warned Professor Wiggly.

"Then we must be quick," said Goldie.
"Let's go!"

They left the library, waving goodbye to the librarian. Ava held the magic music book tightly in her paw.

"What instruments do we need, Ava?" asked Jess. "You're our expert."

Ava's fur fluffed up in pride. "The book says we need a stringed instrument like a harp. And a drum. And a flute, of course."

"We'll start with your flute, Ava," said Goldie. "Let's go and get a reed from Willowtree

River."

They'd just stepped among the trees when they heard a deafening KWARK!

Ava dropped the music book in alarm. The next second Banjo swooped down and snatched it in his beak.

"Give that back!" yelled Ava, leaping in the air to catch the book.

Jess and Lily raced after Banjo, but he was too fast. Soon he'd disappeared among the trees.

"Professor Wiggly's magic music has gone," cried Ava. "What are we going to do now?"

## CHAPTER FOUR

# Find the Instruments!

Jess folded her arms, looking determined. "Don't worry, Ava," she said. "We'll get the music back. But first let's make the new instruments."

"I hope we can do it in time," said Ava fearfully.

"We will," declared Lily. "Come on."

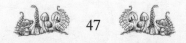

They ran through the forest. Mrs
Longwhiskers the rabbit flapped her
apron in surprise as they raced past the
Toadstool Café. Soon they came to
Willowtree River.

The sparkling water bubbled and
gurgled between the banks. Tall, straight
reeds grew along the edge of the water.

Mr and Mrs Featherbill
the ducks waved to
them from their pretty
blue barge as they
floated by.

Ava searched carefully

through the reeds. At last she chose one and showed the others. "This is just right," she exclaimed. "Straight and hollow." She fiddled with it for a couple of minutes, hollowing it out and adding holes with her sharp little claws. "I don't know if this is going to work," she muttered.

"Try it," said Goldie encouragingly.

Ava blew into it. A sweet, clear note rang out. She looked astonished. "It sounds quite nice!" she cried.

"Perfect!" said Jess. "We knew you

could do it, Ava!"

"AK, AK, AK!" A loud chuckling filled the air.

"That came from the reeds," said Ava in surprise.

Jess noticed that one of the reeds was pink with a knobbly knee! "Banjo!" she shouted. "This could be our chance to get the magic music back."

"It's not Banjo," came a voice. "It's a reed – a pink one. KWARK!"

Banjo's bright tail feathers popped into view.

"We know it's you, Banjo," said Goldie.

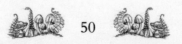

50

"What are you doing here?"

Banjo flapped on to the bank. "Spying on you," he screeched.

"You're not very good at it," said Jess.

"Yes I am." Banjo stamped up and down the bank, squawking crossly.

Lily, Jess, Goldie and Ava got into a huddle. They tried to take no notice of the flamingo, but Banjo was deafening.

"Banjo hasn't got the music book with

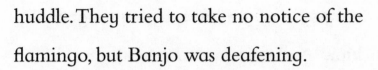

him," said Ava, disappointed.

"We'll get it back," said Lily. "Grizelda isn't going to beat us."

"Well said," declared Goldie. "Now for our harp. We need some strings."

They walked away from the river, searching among the giant toadstools and flowers. Banjo kept butting in rudely between them and charging off, laughing.

"Flower stems will be too floppy for harp strings," said Ava, trying to ignore him. "And strips of bark are too hard."

The girls noticed that her voice had

 52

suddenly grown
fainter.

"Are you all
right, Ava?" asked
Jess. "You're speaking very quietly."

Ava's eyes widened with shock.

"Grizelda's evil spell is spreading," said
Goldie. Her voice was fading too. "Just

like Professor Wiggly
said it would."

Banjo was
perched on a branch
above them. "Your
voices won't come

back." He swooped down towards them.

*BOOM! BANG!* He crashed into a toadstool. "Yow!" he wailed, clutching his leg. "YOWWWWWW!"

Lily and Jess couldn't bear to see any animal in pain – even one who was helping Grizelda.

"Poor Banjo!" gasped Jess. "He's hurt himself!"

# CHAPTER FIVE

# A Special Harp

Banjo sat on the ground, shrieking at the top of his voice.

"Show us your leg, Banjo," said Jess, running over and kneeling next to him.

"What are you going to do?" wailed Banjo.

"We'll make you better," explained Lily.

Banjo stuck out his poorly leg. It was red and sore.

Ava cringed. "What a nasty graze. My mummy always gives me a cobweb plaster from Get-Well Grove when I hurt myself like that."

"That's a long way off," said Jess.

"I know where else we can get one," said Lily. "From Sidney the spider!"

"Good idea," exclaimed Goldie. "We're very close to the Kindness Tree."

The Kindness Tree was where Ivy the good witch lived with her blue spider, Sidney. Sidney used his special webs to help the animals of the forest. But he hadn't always been so kind. Not long ago, he and Ivy had been Grizelda's helpers!

"We'd better hurry," said Jess, "or our voices will be gone before we can ask him for help."

"I can't hurry," cried Banjo. "My leg hurts too much. YOWWWWW!"

"Don't worry, Banjo," said Jess. "We'll carry you."

Lily and Jess linked hands to make a seat for the poor flamingo to sit on. Goldie and Ava led the way through the forest. It was already so much quieter than it had been when Lily and Jess arrived.

They soon came to the Kindness Tree. Sidney was busy weaving a beautiful web across the tree's branches whilst Ivy sat underneath, plaiting her long blue hair.

"Hello, Lily and
Jess," she said. Her voice was
quiet, just like theirs. "What's happened
to that poor flamingo?"

"Banjo's hurt his leg, Ivy," Lily
explained. "Please,
Sidney, could you
make a cobweb
plaster?"

They looked
hopefully at

Sidney. The spider scurried across his web and the word "Yes" appeared in a bright silver thread. He scuttled down and began to spin a small cobweb on a nearby starberry bush.

"Sidney's lost his voice and I have no idea why," said Ivy, worried. "Mine's getting quieter – and yours are faint too."

"Grizelda's trying to take every sound away from the forest," said Jess.

"That's awful!" gasped Ivy.

The girls told Ivy and Sidney about their quest to make new musical instruments and reverse Grizelda's horrible magic.

"You always help us when we need it," said the good witch gratefully.

She pointed a long finger at Sidney's shimmering cobweb. Pretty blue sparkles sprinkled themselves over it. She handed the web to the girls.

Lily wrapped the cobweb plaster gently around Banjo's leg.

"WOW!" shouted Banjo. He gave a beaming smile. "It worked. My leg's better! Look." He danced around to show that it was healed. "Thank you, Sidney. Thank you, Ivy." Then he hung his head. "You've all been so kind," he boomed, looking embarrassed. "And I was really mean. I'm not going to help Grizelda any more."

Everyone cheered, as loudly as they were able to.

Jess gazed at the web. Sidney's strands were thin but they were very strong. They reminded her of something. "These look like the strings of an instrument," she said.

"You're right," gasped Ava.

"Could you make us some special strings for a harp, Sidney?" Lily asked the spider.

Sidney spun the words "Of course!"

"I'll find something for the frame," said Ava. She ran off towards a weeping willow, but within minutes she was back holding a curved branch. Sidney got to work and soon the wood was bound with silvery strings.

"Now for a little something extra!" declared Ivy. She gently stroked the strings, covering them in blue sparkles.

"Now it will always play beautiful music." She smiled.

When Ava plucked the harp they could just hear its faint tune.

"It's wonderful!" said Ava in a whisper. "Thank you both."

"We're glad to help," said Ivy. "Oh dear, my voice is almost gone!"

"We must hurry," croaked Lily.

They waved goodbye to Ivy and
Sidney and walked back into the trees.
But then they stopped in dismay. The
forest, usually so full of lovely sounds, was
hushed and still.

"I can't hear the river any more," said
Goldie faintly.

"And the birds aren't singing either,"
breathed Jess. She gazed up to the trees.
Finches and wagtails were sitting sadly
in the branches, their beaks opening and
closing silently.

"Why are you all whispering?" asked
Banjo. "Is it a game?"

"No, it's not," wheezed Goldie. "It's Grizelda's wicked spell. But we're going to beat it."

"Kwark!" cried Banjo, opening his beak as wide as he could. "My voice is croaky too."

Lily and Jess could hear that Banjo was right. Even though he was still loud, he wasn't as deafening as before.

"Oh dear," squeaked Ava. "We still have to find a drum – but where from?"

Everyone thought hard.

"I've got it!" squawked Banjo, making them jump. "When I tripped over that

toadstool, it went *BOOM! BANG!* Just
like a drum."

"You're right, Banjo!" whispered Lily.

"I'll fetch one!" croaked Goldie. She
bounded off through the trees.

"The music book!" Jess tried to say. Her
words were just a whisper now. "Banjo
took it when we left the library."

"You'll give it to us, won't you, Banjo?"
said Ava in a faraway voice.

But the flamingo hid his head under his
wing. "I can't," came his muffled reply.

"Have you lost the book?" whispered
Lily gently.

"No." Banjo's head slowly appeared. "I gave it to Grizelda. WAAAA!"

Lily and Jess looked at each other in horror. How could they save Friendship Forest now?

CHAPTER SIX

# A Very Special Song

Goldie came rushing back, carrying a toadstool. "Here's the drum," she wheezed. She beat a rhythm on it. Lily and Jess could just hear the faint sound.

"That's wonderful," Jess said in a tiny voice. "But we have a problem."

She told Goldie about the missing book

 69

of magical music.

Ava suddenly waved her paws. "We can play my song!" The others bent to catch her words. "Professor Wiggly said the music must use every note in the forest. My song used nearly all the different notes! I can add the rest. It won't be perfect, but I hope it's good enough to break the spell."

"Brilliant, Ava," whispered Lily.

"You play the drum, Goldie," squeaked Ava. "Jess, you take the harp. I can play the flute and Lily, can you sing?"

"Teach me the words," breathed Lily.

Ava tried to sing the song. Lily listened closely to learn the words.

"We're ready," croaked Jess. "One, two, three, four!"

They began to play. The music sounded lovely but very faint. Lily got ready to sing. But no words came.

She tried again. Nothing happened. She pointed to her mouth, shaking her head.

Lily, Jess, Goldie and Ava looked at each other. Were they too late? Had their voices disappeared for good?

"What's happening?" yelped Banjo.

"Why aren't you singing?"

Lily realised that Banjo still had some of his voice. He was quieter than before, but they could still hear him. He could sing the song!

She pointed to him and silently pretended to sing.

Banjo put his head to one side, puzzled.

But the others had understood. They all pointed to Banjo while Lily pretended to sing again.

Banjo suddenly beamed. "You want me to sing!" he exclaimed. "I can do that. I was listening really hard so I know

the song already."

The band struck up again. Banjo sang

the words as loudly as he could.

> "*I love to play,*
>
> *And sing my song,*
>
> *In Friendship Forest,*
>
> *All day long.*
>
> *And when I sing,*
>
> *With all my friends,*
>
> *I hope the music,*
>
> *Never ends!*"

At first the instruments couldn't be

heard, but suddenly Lily caught the faint

beat of Goldie's drum. Now she could

hear Ava's flute and Jess's harp. At last, beautiful notes came out loud and clear and the drumbeat echoed through the trees.

Ava stopped playing. "Listen," she cried.

Wonderful forest sounds burst out all around.

"I can hear the leaves rustling," exclaimed Jess, putting down her harp. "And the river flowing."

"Our voices are back too!" cried Lily.

"And the birdsong is lovely," said Ava. "It's like music."

"It is music," said Goldie happily. "The music of Friendship Forest."

"WE'VE BROKEN THE SPELL," boomed Banjo. "HOORAY!"

They all joined together in a big hug.

"KWARK!" squawked Banjo happily as they squeezed him tight.

"It's nearly time for the concert!" said Ava suddenly. "We must get back to the school."

"Goodbye," said Banjo, his beak drooping sadly. "Have a lovely time."

Ava looked up at him. "Banjo, would you like to come too? After all, you helped us save the sounds of Friendship Forest."

"KWARK!" yelled Banjo in happiness. "I mean, yes please!"

They hurried off to Spelltop School,

77

all singing Ava's song at the tops of their
voices as they ran.

CHAPTER SEVEN

# The Nasty Spell is Broken

The girls burst into the school hall, with Goldie, Ava and Banjo close behind.

The orchestra were excitedly showing each other their sheets of music and trying their instruments. The notes were back on the pages and the instruments

sounded beautiful
again. Lily and
Jess ran over
to Professor
Gogglewing.
He beamed
at them.

"How can I thank you for defeating
Grizelda?" he exclaimed.

"You don't need to," said Lily. "We're
just pleased that Ava's wonderful music
broke the spell."

"She's a fine musician," said the kindly
old headmaster.

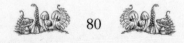

Ava gave a shy grin.

"Is it time for the concert?" came a voice behind them. Professor Cutiepaws burst out from behind the stage curtains. She tripped over a music stand, then crashed into the cymbals, sending them flying, and fell off the stage. "Oh dear, I'm such a clumsy cupcake."

Lily and Jess helped her up.

"Are you all right?" gasped Ava.

"Yes, kittykins," gushed Professor Cutiepaws. "And ready to conduct the orchestra and your lovely song." She looked around, her white whiskers

twitching. "As soon as I can lay my hands
– oops, silly me, I mean my paws – on my
baton. I can't possibly conduct without it."
She scurried out of the hall, poking her
head into every corner as she went.

Lily, Jess and Ava began searching too.
Ava suddenly gave a purr of excitement
and pointed under a chair. She'd found
Professor Cutiepaws's baton! The girls
cheered.

But as Ava picked up the baton, smelly
yellow sparks shot out from one end! It
jumped from her grip and hit the floor
with a clatter. The little kitten leapt back

from the baton in fright.

Jess stood on it to stop it writhing all over the floor. "Smelly yellow sparks mean one thing," she said grimly. "This isn't a baton. It's Grizelda's wand!"

"So that's what ruined the music!" exclaimed Lily.

Professor Cutiepaws came rushing back. "Frizzling furballs!" she said, pointing at the wriggling baton. "Is that—?"

"It belongs to Grizelda," Goldie told her. "When you used it to conduct the orchestra, it cast her wicked spell."

The white cat's paws flew to her mouth. "Goodness!" she cried. "That nasty witch used me for her trick. I'll take the baton so it can't be used again."

"I've got a better idea," said Jess. "We'll break it."

She picked up the wand and snapped it in half. It split with a big crack and another shower of smelly sparks.

"Now it can't make any more bad magic," said Lily. "Well done, Jess."

Professor Cutiepaws had a strange scowl on her face.

"Are you all right, Professor Cutiepaws?" Jess asked.

Professor Cutiepaws quickly changed her frown into a beaming smile. "Oh! Yes! I was just thinking how awful it would be if you or any of the little animals had been harmed by that horrible magic."

"We'll bury the pieces after the concert," said Jess, tucking the broken wand under her arm.

Lily was sure she saw a horrified look flit over Professor Cutiepaws's face. But, in the twinkling of an eye, the white cat was smiling again.

Professor Gogglewing waddled over. "I'd be delighted if you'd use my baton instead, Professor Cutiepaws."

"Thank you, Headmaster," gushed the teacher. She suddenly staggered.

"Wiggling whiskers, I feel dizzy. I can't conduct the concert."

"Can we help?" asked the girls.

"No thank you, sugarlumps," said Professor Cutiepaws. "I just need to lie down, all alone, all by myself."

With that, she rushed from the hall.

"I hate to say this," Lily murmured to Jess and Goldie, "but there's something odd about Professor Cutiepaws."

"I agree," said Jess. "She seemed really upset when we broke Grizelda's wand."

"You don't think she's helping Grizelda, do you?" whispered Lily.

"No one so nice would help that terrible witch," gasped Goldie.

"I hope you're right, Goldie," said Jess in a low voice.

Professor Gogglewing waddled over. "We'll need a new conductor," he said. He put a wing round Ava and whispered something in her ear.

The little kitten's eyes shone and her soft, pale fur fluffed up happily. "The headmaster has asked me to conduct the concert!" she said breathlessly.

"AMAZING!" squawked Banjo, deafening everyone.

Lily and Jess beamed, while Banjo ran round them in dizzy circles.

"But if I'm conducting, someone else must sing the words of my song," said Ava. "And I know just who to ask."

"Who's that?" asked Lily.

"Banjo," said Ava with a big grin.

The young flamingo skidded to a halt.

 89

"Would you like that, Banjo?" said Jess, smiling in encouragement.

"YES, I WOULD!" squawked Banjo in delight. "KWARK! I CAN'T WAIT!"

## CHAPTER EIGHT

# A Wonderful Concert

Lily, Jess and Goldie sat in the front row,
ready for the concert. Every animal in
the forest had come to listen. Mr and Mrs
Muddlepup were in the row behind, next
to the Nibblesqueaks, who waved happily
at their three daughters on the stage.
Everyone knew Lily and Jess, and they

all gave them big, beaming smiles as they took their seats.

"This is Mr and Mrs Fluffyface," said Goldie, introducing the proud cats sitting beside her. "They're Ava's parents."

"We've got our paws crossed for Ava," said Mrs Fluffyface. "We know she wants everything to be perfect."

"But we've told her everyone will love it anyway," added Mr Fluffyface. "She's such a clever kitten!"

Professor Gogglewing waddled on to the stage and held up his wings for quiet. "Welcome to Spelltop School," he announced, warmly. "And now open your ears for a wonderful musical treat."

Ava raised the baton and the orchestra started playing. Lily and Jess looked at each other happily. The beautiful sounds of Friendship Forest were safe again.

When it was time for Ava's song, Banjo came forward, his wings fluttering

eagerly. The orchestra struck up and the audience gasped at the wonderful notes that filled the hall. Banjo opened his beak wide and belted out the words at the top of his voice. It was a bit loud and he didn't sing it perfectly, but he was having so much fun that everyone loved it. The whole crowd joined in and sang along.

When it was over they cheered and clapped and called for it to be played again. Ava purred with pleasure as she raised the baton.

And this time Banjo sang even louder!

The audience clapped until their hands and paws and wings ached. Mr and Mrs Fluffyface glowed with pride at their clever daughter. Ava rushed down to give them a hug.

"Thank goodness we broke Grizelda's spell," said Jess, watching Ava chattering excitedly to her mum and dad after the concert.

"Now we'd better bury the wand before it can do any more harm," said Lily.

She and Jess fetched spades from the

 95

school greenhouse and went with Goldie,
Ava and Banjo to the flowerbed beside
the library.

"I can't wait to be rid of this horrible
thing," said Goldie, as they dug a hole.

"Oh no," said Jess, glancing up.
"We need to hurry. Look!" An orb
of yellow-green light came shooting
into the playground. It stopped beside
them, showering foul-smelling sparks
everywhere as Grizelda appeared.

"Quick," said Goldie, piling earth on
top of the wand. "We must get this buried
before she can snatch it."

Lily quickly patted the earth down and they stood to face the witch.

"Go away," said Jess. "Your nasty spell hasn't worked."

"There are always other spells," snapped Grizelda.

"And we'll spoil every one," Lily told her firmly.

Grizelda gave a shriek of rage. She stamped her foot so hard that the heel of

her boot snapped off.

"You foolish girls may have won this time," she screeched in fury, hobbling about on her one heel. "But I'll come up with a new plan, just you wait and see. Every animal will be driven from Friendship Forest. And I will be all alone, all by myself."

Banjo flapped out of the school hall, with Ava by his side. They both looked scared but that didn't stop them rushing over to join the girls and Goldie.

Ava gave an angry miaow. "Keep away from our school, you nasty witch."

98

"You haven't seen the last of me,"
Grizelda warned. She pointed a bony
finger at the young flamingo. "Let's go,
Banjo."

Banjo stalked right up to the witch.
Lily and Jess held their breath. He'd said
he wasn't going to help Grizelda any
more. Was he about to change his mind?

"I'm not leaving," squawked Banjo.

The girls gave a cheer.

"What?" snapped Grizelda.

"I'm staying at Spelltop School," said
Banjo. "No one is mean to me here. I'm
not just a noisy flamingo. I'm a proper

singer and everyone likes me."

Grizelda's eyes blazed as her face turned as purple as her tunic. "I don't need you any more," she screeched. "I've still got one flamingo servant left, and he's the best of the bunch." She disappeared in another shower of stinky sparks.

"Now it's our turn to go," said Jess.

She and Lily gave Ava and Banjo a hug. Banjo was so pleased he did a somersault.

"Come on, Ava," he called to the little kitten. "Let's go and make up a new song together."

"That would be lovely," she purred. "Goodbye, Lily and Jess. And thank you for saving the sounds of Friendship Forest."

The girls waved goodbye and Goldie led them to the Friendship Tree.

"We'll be back the moment Grizelda tries any more of her nasty tricks," Jess promised, as they reached the tree in the

centre of the forest.

"Do keep an eye on Professor Cutiepaws," said Lily. "Just to be sure."

"I will," said Goldie as they hugged goodbye.

Goldie touched the bark and the magic door appeared. Lily and Jess stepped through the shimmering light and into the spring sunshine of Brightley Meadow.

"Let's check on the little egg," said Jess.

"An *eggcellent* idea," joked Lily.

They raced back to the Helping Paw Wildlife Hospital. The beautiful blue egg was lying under its warm lamp.

"Listen!" gasped Jess. "Something's happening."

They heard a soft *tap, tap, tap* and a tiny crack appeared in the shell. It grew and grew, and soon the girls could see the tip of a yellow beak appear through the hole.

"Come on, little chick," whispered Lily. "You can do it."

The shell fell into two halves and the chick burst out. Its eyes were closed and it was covered in tufts of white fluff.

"It's so tiny," breathed Jess.

"And so cute," added Lily.

The new baby opened its beak and

began to chirp – loudly!

"That reminds me of Banjo," giggled Jess.

Mrs Hart came in.

"Hello, little one," she cooed. "It's a song thrush," she told the girls. "It'll make lovely music when it's older."

Lily whispered in Jess's ear. "Just like a clever little kitten we know."

The End

Far away in Friendship Forest, Lily and Jess are working hard at the magical Spelltop School. But behind all the enchanted fun, there is dark magic brewing ... and the girls think they know where it's coming from ...

Can cuddlesome koala Ella Snugglepaw help them save the school once and for all?

Find out in the next Magic Animal Friends book,

# Ella Snugglepaw's Big Cuddle

Turn over for a sneak peek ...

Lily Hart took a handful of curly kale leaves to her best friend, Jess Forester. "The guinea pigs will love this!" she said.

The girls were outside the Helping Paw Wildlife Hospital, which Lily's parents ran in a barn in their garden. Jess and her family lived right opposite Lily, and both girls loved caring for the animal patients. Today they were putting feed in the outside runs where rabbits, guinea pigs, squirrels and other creatures lived once they were on the mend.

Jess's tabby kitten, Pixie, ran to meet Mr Hart, who was bringing a bale of straw for bedding. But then she spotted something interesting in the hedge and touched it with her little pink nose.

Lily went to have a look, too. "Pixie's found a weird leafy thing hanging from a twig," she called to the others.

"It's a chrysalis," Mr Hart said. "One day it will become a butterfly."

"Wow!" said Jess, peering at the chrysalis too. It looked like a pea pod – green and closed up. When she touched it very gently, it was hard like a nut. "I can't believe a strange-looking thing like that can become something so beautiful!"

As Mr Hart headed for the stable, a flash of gold among some roses caught Lily's eye. "Look!" she called. "A butterfly!"

Jess grinned. "That's no butterfly. It's Goldie!"

A beautiful cat with golden fur and eyes as green as summer leaves ran to press against their legs, purring. Goldie was the girls' special friend. She took them on amazing adventures in a magical place called Friendship Forest, where all the animals lived in little cottages or dens. And, best of all, they could all talk!

Goldie suddenly darted towards Brightley Stream, at the bottom of the garden.

"Come on!" said Jess. "She's taking us to Friendship Forest!"

Read

# Ella Snugglepaw's Big Cuddle

to find out what happens next!

# Jess and Lily's Animal Facts

Lily and Jess love lots of different animals –
both in Friendship Forest
and in the real world.

Here are their top facts about

## KITTENS
like Ava Fluffyface:

- Cats need lots of sleep – between 13 and 14 hours a day!

- A group of cats is called a clowder, a male cat is called a tom, a female cat is called a molly or queen

- Kittens are born with their eyes closed, and with tightly sealed ears. When they are between 7 and 10 days old they open their eyes for the very first time

- When a kitten is born, it spends several weeks just sleeping and feeding

- A kitten becomes a cat after about a year

**Magic**
**Animal Friends**
*Can you keep the secret?*

There's lots of fun for everyone at
**www.magicanimalfriends.com**

Play games and explore the secret world of
Friendship Forest, where animals can talk!

# Join the
# Magic Animal Friends Club!

⭐ Special competitions ⭐
⭐ Exclusive content ⭐
⭐ All the latest Magic Animal Friends news! ⭐

To join the Club, simply go to

**www.magicanimalfriends.com/join-our-club/**